A
LITTLE BOOK
OF
TRAIN
TALES

ILLUSTRATED BY
GRAHAME CORBETT

HUTCHINSON
LONDON · MELBOURNE · AUCKLAND · JOHANNESBURG

Produced by Templar Publishing Ltd,
107 High Street, Dorking, Surrey RH4 1QA,
for Hutchinson Children's Books

First published 1987 by Hutchinson Children's Books
An imprint of Century Hutchinson Ltd,
Brookmount House, 62-65 Chandos Place, Covent Garden,
London WC2N 4NW

Century Hutchinson Group (Australia) Pty Ltd,
16-22 Church Street, Hawthorn, Melbourne, Victoria 3122

Century Hutchinson Group (NZ) Ltd,
32-34 View Road, PO Box 40-086, Glenfield, Auckland 10

Century Hutchinson Group (SA) Pty Ltd,
PO Box 337, Bergvlei 2012, South Africa

Set in Times Roman by Templar Type

British Library Cataloging in Publication Data

A Little book of train stories.
    1. Children's stories, English
    I. Corbett, Grahame
    823'.01'089282 [J]   PZ5
ISBN 0-09-171770-1

Colour separations by Positive Colour Ltd, Maldon, Essex
Printed and bound by L.E.G.O., Vincenza, Italy

Contents

The Little Green Train

by Sally Sheringham

The Little Green Train lived in an attic. It was a nice, cobwebby attic with a sloping ceiling and a little window that let in the sun in the afternoon. The Little Green Train didn't have a shed to sleep in like proper trains. He slept instead, in the cardboard box that he had arrived in from the shop. His owner, John, slept in the room below.

Every day John came up to the attic to play. He put the Little Green Train on the track. Round and round he went: clackerty-clack, clackerty-clack, clackerty-clack.

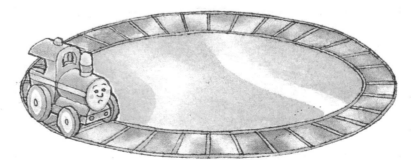

After a while John stopped coming to the attic. He had got bored with the Little Green Train just going round and round. Secretly, the Little Green Train was beginning to feel rather bored, too. Besides, going round and round made him feel rather dizzy.

"I don't want to spend the rest of my life in a cobwebby attic just going round and round, like a goldfish in a bowl," he thought. "I want to see the big outside world and travel past stations and under bridges like a proper train."

So, one day, when the house was quiet, he bumperty-bumped down the stairs, and clackerty-clacked out of the front door.

As he went through the gate, the Little Green Train whistled to himself. So far so good – now to find some proper trains!

He huffed and puffed down the road and across fields, hills and dales. After a while, he met a very large animal. "Excuse me," said the

Little Green Train. "Could you tell me the way to the station?" But the very large animal just went "Moo".

The Little Green Train's wheels were begining to feel sore. He was not used to so much travelling. At times he just wished he was back in his peaceful, cobwebby attic.

Suddenly, just ahead of him, he saw the silver glint of a proper railway track. How wide it was! The Little Green Train began to follow it. Then the ground began to rumble and grumble beneath him. There was a great screaming sound and an enormous monster thundered towards him, swooshing and whooshing, rattling and belching.

For a moment the Little Green Train thought he was going to die of fright. Then he realised that the monster was – a proper train! It was at least a hundred times bigger than he was, and a hundred times faster.

"Oh dear," thought the Little Green Train. "No wonder John is bored with me. I can only ever be small and slow." And a fat tear rolled down his green paint.

The proper train stopped. "Are you lost?" it asked. The Little Green Train nodded. "Hop in, I'll take you home," said the proper train kindly.

What an exciting journey it was! They whooshed and whistled across the fields, under bridges and through tunnels.

"I feel just like a real train!" laughed the Little Green Train. The proper train and its driver laughed, too.

When they got back to the station, the proper train said goodbye and its driver carried the Little Green Train back home. There was John, looking anxiously out of the window.

"Oh, Little Green Train, I've been looking everywhere for you, " he cried, picking him up and giving him a big hug. "It's my birthday today, and my aunt has given me a new train set. But it's useless without you. Oh, I'm so pleased you've come home!"

The Little Green Train was pleased to be home, too. And when he saw the attic, he could hardly believe his eyes. The old circular track had gone. There, in its place, was a shiny new track that ran all the way round the room. It had sidings, signal boxes and points. There was a station and model trees, a bridge to go over, a bridge to go under, a long tunnel, two stations – and a proper train shed for him to sleep in! He had a long line of freshly painted carriages and goods waggons, and even a guard's van.

"This beats the big outside world, any day!" laughed the Little Green Train, as he clackerty-clacked, whooshed and whistled around his new track – just like a proper train!

The Ghost Train

by Philip Steele

A lot of funny things happen in Winkleton. A lot of very *peculiar* things. It looks such a sleepy little town. But the people there are – well, peculiar.

Mister Buffer was the station master at Winkleton Station. He collected the tickets. He polished the big clock. He had a red lantern which meant STOP and a green lantern which meant GO. When the midnight train came down the line, it was Mister Buffer who had to open the gates of the level crossing.

"Why has it always got to be *me*?" he grumbled, one dark and gloomy night. "Why do *I* have to freeze? Everyone else is tucked up in bed. Why do *I* have to stay up – on *Hallowe'en* of all nights?…"

Hallowe'en! Of course, it was Hallowe'en. When witches and hobgoblins prowl around. Mister Buffer shivered. He was just going in, to warm his toes by the fire, when he heard a faraway noise. Whooo-whooooo!

"That's odd," thought Mister Buffer. "That's a train whistle. But it's far too early for the midnight train!"

Chu-chu-chu-chu-chooo – whooo-whooooooo! It was getting nearer! Mister Buffer peered down the track. What was that glow in the tunnel? Clankety-*clank*! Clickety-clackety-*clank*! Whooo-whooooOOOO!!! A hideous steam train came shuddering down the track.

There was a skull-and-crossbones on the smokebox. It was covered in dust and cobwebs. Tatters and rags streamed from the windows. And it glowed, a pale blue.

Mister Buffer shouted and waved his lantern. "Stop! Stop, I tell you!"

There was a screeching of brakes. Steam hissed across the platform. When it cleared, Mister Buffer could see long, bony fingers gripping the driver's window.

Over the edge of the cab rose a sickly white face. It was as round as the full moon. Its eyes glowed like burning coals. It grinned and grinned, and let out a horrible, wailing laugh.

"Hee-hee-heeeeeeeeeee! I'm Ebenezer and I'm a spook, and you can't catch me-he-heeee!"

"Oh yes I can," said Mister Buffer boldly.

"Oh no you can't," cackled the spook.

Mister Buffer was cross.

"The gate is shut on the level crossing, see. So you *can't* get through."

"That's not *fair*," wailed Ebenezer. "I'm a busy spook. I've got a lot of people to frighten tonight. Do you think I enjoy hanging around in draughty stations? Do you think I like driving a train which goes clank-clank all the time? Boo-hoooo!"

To Mister Buffer's surprise, two large tears rolled down Ebenezer's face. He began to feel sorry for the spook.

"Well, I don't like draughty stations either," he said. "Why don't you get down off that train? We can sit by my fire and have a chat."

Now, if you had peered through the window of Winkleton Station on that dark and gloomy night, you would have seen a strange sight. The station master and the spook were talking and talking, like old friends. Then they came back outside. Mister Buffer opened the crossing gate – and climbed into the train with Ebenezer! As the train drove away, they were cackling with laughter! What on earth was going on?

The next day dawned. It was a clear autumn morning, and the fair was coming to Winkleton. Lorries and caravans filled the street. Soon there were coconut-shies and round-abouts and all the fun of the fair. In the corner of one field was a large, mysterious tent. It had never been seen before. A crowd of children soon gathered around it, and a little man with a moustache appeared.

"Roll up! Roll up!" he shouted. "Get the fright of your lives! Roll up for a ride on THE GHOST TRAIN!!!"

"Why, it's Mr Buffer!" cried one of the children.

And so it was. The children flocked in and Mister Buffer rode round and round in the train all day, while Ebenezer made spooky noises and poked them and flapped cobwebs in their faces. It was a hoot! At the end of the day, Ebenezer and Mister Buffer counted up the money.

"Hooray, we're in business!" said the spook gleefully.

And so they were. But then the people from Winkleton always did get up to some very peculiar things...

Grandma Goosegog's Birthday Treat

by Philip Steele

Grandma Goosegog had lived in Station Road all her life. Everybody knew her. She was the little old lady with snowy white hair, and specs on the end of her nose. Her house was right next to the railway station – but do you know what? She had never been on a train in her life.

Soon it was to be Grandma Goosegog's one hundredth birthday. Everyone in the street agreed on one thing – she had to have a special party. But what could they give her as a present? She already had a sewing box and a silver thimble, and a little cat called Charlie.

"I have an idea," said the boy who lived next door. "We could buy her a ticket for a train ride!"

Everyone thought this was a very good idea. She could ride all the way to Steepleton, and *really* travel in style!

The day of Grandma Goosegog's birthday dawned. Everyone came to her party and said, "Many happy returns!" or "You don't look a day over 21!" – which made the old lady laugh and laugh. She blew out the candles on her cake (there weren't *quite* a hundred of them) and then her special treat was announced.

Grandma Goosegog was delighted.

"A train ride! After all these years! How exciting! Thank you, everyone."

A band was playing outside her house, as she was helped across the road and on to the station platform. The station master shook her by the hand, and the engine driver climbed down from his cab and opened a carriage door for her.

Now, in all the excitement, Grandma Goosegog had lost her specs. Instead of getting into the carriage, she climbed into the driver's cab!

"Now then, where's that dratted door handle?" she muttered to herself, and pressed a button saying DIESEL ON. Then she tried another button. Whooooooooooosh! The train thundered away from the platform at high speed. The engine driver ran down the track. The people from the street ran after him, still wearing their party hats.

"Come back! Come back!" they yelled. But the train disappeared into a tunnel. The station master ran for the telephone. He called the signal men and he called Steepleton Station.

"Beware! Beware! There's a runaway train!" he shouted into the receiver.

Grandma Goosegog was having a whale of a time. This really was something special! Her woolly scarf streamed out behind her. Ratatat-ratatat-ratatatat! went the wheels on the track. The train went faster and faster. It flew past a farmyard. Geese cackled and hens squawked. The train roared over a level crossing. "How nice of all those policemen to be waving at me!"

thought Grandma. She waved back graciously, feeling rather like the queen.

"*Brake, fast!*" shouted a railway worker.

"Oh, I've had my breakfast, thanks!" she shouted from the window. "And my lunch, too!" Just then Steepleton Station came into view.

"It looks very empty," Grandma said thought-fully. "I wonder why those people are hiding over there? Whoops-a-daisy!" The train went through the buffers and the ticket barrier, and crashed through the brick wall at the back of the station. It clattered down the High Street

and into a laundry. Out it came again, covered in sheets. Wham! It shot through a cafe, and came out covered in steak-and-kidney pudding. Thunk! It ploughed into a bridge and toppled into the river.

The fire brigade soon arrived, then the man from the cafe, the woman from the laundry, the workers from the railway, the farmer with the geese and, last of all, the engine driver and all Grandma's friends from Station Road.

"Has anyone seen Grandma Goosegog?" they called anxiously.

A small voice was heard from behind the train: "Oh, have you come along? Delightful! Just fancy, I'm getting a free swim, too!" And Grandma Goosegog came into view, swimming down the river and covered in waterweed. She told them it was her best birthday ever.

"I think for your next birthday, we'll knit you something instead," said the engine driver. "A nice tea-cosy, perhaps."

"Thanks all the same," replied Grandma, "but I've got a tea-cosy already. Now did you happen to know that I've never yet been on an *aeroplane*?…"

The Wizard and the Weasel

by Philip Steele

There was once a funny old steam engine. It huffed and puffed, clinked and clanked, and it frightened the cows in the field when it went *toot-toot*! The name on its brass plate was *Wizard*. Its driver was called Billy Binns, and *he* said it was the best little engine in the world. Everyone loved the *Wizard*.

Everyone, that is, except Billy's boss, Mr Snarkey.

"That precious engine of yours is too old!" he told Billy one morning. "It's been rattling around our railway for forty years, and it's not going to rattle around any more. I think I'll get one of those nice new diesel express trains!"

Billy could hardly believe his ears.

"A diesel? You can't do that, Mr Snarkey! They're not proper trains! And the *Wizard* is as fast as any of them when it gets going."

"Billy," said Mr Snarkey. "Nobody can say I'm not a fair man. If your *Wizard* can go faster than a diesel express, we'll keep the old engine on. We'll have a race and see who wins!"

"But what if the *Wizard* loses?" asked Billy.

"Then it will have to go," said Snarkey. "We can't have these silly old steam engines cluttering up our nice new stations!"

Billy Binns polished the *Wizard* until it gleamed. He painted the cab green and gold. He oiled every part of it. He'd show them!

On the morning of the big race a large, grimy diesel engine chug-chugged into the shed in a cloud of smelly smoke. It didn't have a name, just a number on its side. Its driver was a thin fellow who looked like a weasel.

"Did you ever see the likes?" chuckled Billy. "A weasel driving a diesel! Let's hope he goes pop!" And he started to whistle 'Pop Goes the Weasel'.

Along came Mr Snarkey in his bowler hat. He pulled a watch from his waistcoat pocket.

"Right, lads. When I wave, off you go. The first train to Wigglesworth Station is the winner."

He raised a green flag high in the air. Down it went! WHOOOSH! Steam billowed across the tracks. Chuff-chuff-chuff-CHUFF! Off went the little *Wizard* and off went the great big diesel.

Now the race was a sight to see. First one was in front, then the other. The wheels clacked on the tracks and the wind blew in their faces. Sparks were flying! They passed through the village and everyone cheered. They went through a long black tunnel. They tore past a signal box and the signal man shouted:

"Come on Billy! Up the *Wizard*! You can make it!"

But when they rounded Willow Bend, a very sad sight caught Billy's eye. There, by the track, was a little boy in tears. Billy slammed on the brakes, but the diesel engine roared past and vanished in the distance.

"What's up, lad?" asked Billy kindly.

"I'm lost!" wailed the little boy. "Boo hoo! My dog ran away and I went to look for him, and I didn't find him, and now I don't know where I am!" He sobbed and sobbed.

"Never mind, laddy," said Billy. "We'll get you home all right. Now you jump up here, and we'll have the train ride of a lifetime! When we get to the station, we'll find your mum and dad. You mustn't hang around railway lines. They're dangerous places!"

The *Wizard* steamed up the track again, and the little boy stopped crying. What a ride! But the fact of the matter was, when the *Wizard* chuffed into Wigglesworth Station, it was Billy Binns who felt like crying. There was Mr Snarkey shaking the weasel by the hand.

"It's no good, Billy!" he shouted. "You lost the race."

And so indeed he had. The little boy was sent off to his parents, and the poor old *Wizard* was shunted off into a siding. And there it stayed for many a long year. The rain fell down and made it rusty. The paint peeled off, and grass and moss grew over the wheels. Billy Binns moved away and almost everyone forgot the *Wizard*.

But one person didn't forget: the little boy. All his life he remembered his exciting ride on the last of the grand old steam trains. And, do you know? When he grew up, he found the old engine and bought it. He painted it and polished it just like Billy Binns had done, all those years before.

Today you can see the *Wizard* in a railway museum, as smart as the day it was made. And there it will stay, carefully looked after for ever and a day ... long after the smelly old diesel has been sent for scrap, and hammered into dustbin lids!

The Reluctant Train

by Stanley Bates

"The train on Platform Ten is about to depart," boomed the voice over the loudspeaker.

"The train on Platform Ten is *not* about to depart," said the train to himself.

The big iron gates banged shut, leaving some cross passengers behind. The guard closed the train doors. The signal changed from red to green, and the whistle blew. Nothing happened. The guard blew his whistle again – still nothing happened. The train refused to move.

Passengers started to complain, and look out of the windows.

"Why aren't we going? What's happening?"

"What's the matter with this train?"

The guard telephoned through to the driver.

"What's wrong, what's the hold up?" he said.

"Don't know, the train just won't move," came the reply.

The driver got out and looked at the engine. He scratched his head. "Why won't the train go?"

"I won't go," said the train in a whisper, "because I'm bored. Every day it's the same old thing. All I do is carry these people from one station to another, and back again. I see the same faces, the same houses, the same trees, the same everything – I want a change!"

The train thought for a long time, then he said to himself. "I know, I'd much rather be an aeroplane, flying through the sky from one country to another." But then he thought a bit more. "I wouldn't see anything up in the sky, except lots and lots of sky, a cloud maybe and birds, and in any case I don't like heights. No, I don't want to be an aeroplane."

He thought for a while.

"A ship! Yes, a ship! A great big ocean liner, that's what I'd like to be! I'd be very graceful, sailing along on the high seas ... except, I don't like water very much, and there would be so much water all around me – no trees or houses to look at! Oh dear, perhaps being a ship isn't such a good idea after all!"

By this time all the passengers had got out of the train. They were standing on the platform, just looking at the train, and getting very cross. But the train didn't seem to care, he was still thinking what he would rather be.

"A bus! Yes, a shiny red, double-decker bus. That would be much better than being a train, or would it? All day long, I'd hear that bell going ding! ding! – I wouldn't like that. And then, there's all that traffic, stop, go, stop, go! It would take me for ever to get from one place to another. I'd always be late, and then I'd get into trouble. Oh dear! Oh dear! Whatever shall I be? I can't be a car, they're too small. I don't want to be a ghost train – I'd be frightened all the time. And I wouldn't want to be a rocket – I might go up, and never come down again. Bicycles are just silly. So perhaps being a train isn't quite so bad after all."

And at that moment he heard the driver say: "I'll have one last try."

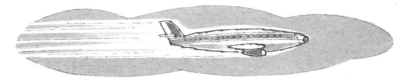

"All right, I'm ready now," said the train. "Let's go!"

"Everybody on the train as quickly as possible!" shouted the guard. "Close all the doors!"

"I think we're moving!"

"Wonder what was wrong?", the train heard the passengers saying.

Soon he was rushing along the track to the next station.

"Good morning trees!" he shouted out as he whizzed by. "Hello houses! Lovely day!"

An aeroplane was flying high, high above the train.

The train looked up and thought, "I would never want to be an aeroplane, it's so very exciting being a train!"